Adventures i

Sh

MW01156005

Pinbeam Books

http://www.pinbeambooks.com

COPYRIGHT PAGE

Technical Details

Landed Alien was published to the Baen Books website (www.baen.com), July 2012

Eleutherios was published to the Baen Books website (www.baen.com), January 2013

The Devil's in the Details is original to this publication

ISBN: 978-1-935224-99-0

Published August 2013 by Pinbeam Books

Pinbeam Books

PO Box 1586

Waterville ME 04903

email info@pinbeambooks.com

Liaden Universe® is a registered trademark

Cover image from JupiterImages

Cover design by Sharon Lee

The Devil's in the Details

Long before we were writers, we were readers: we read and celebrated science fiction as we grew up, absorbing from the literature much of the essence of the field.

One such essence of the field is the tech.

Be it a weapon, a time machine, a ship, or some other type of gadget or gizmo; be it used for good or for evil—SF is about the toys. Not, mind you, *all* about the toys, but the tech is important, and should play a role in any SF story. It may not be the central feature, that tech, but it needs to be there – and yes, sometimes it can be the problem.

But, the problem need not be a weapon. It need not be a self-aware bulldozer. It still can be part of the key and the foundation, it can be as important as the people. It serves man only as long as the people and the tech are working together, with intent. That of course was part of the horror of a famous scene in 2001, where Dave can't get that pod bay door open ... or the threat and menace of all the other errant robots and automatic can-openers* popular across the years.

The tech defines SF; heroes wield it, villains deploy it, masses are crushed beneath, or elevated, by it—but very few want to talk about the most important citizen of any technological society.

The technicians.

Since the Liaden Universe® is not immune to technology, it is not immune to those so very important, though largely invisible, cogs in the wheel of technological society; the often-unsung heroes who keep the tech running.

The two stories here, different as they are, deal with those heroes who not only know which screwdriver to use, but have it on their belt. Those who know, as much as anyone—and more than some—that the devil is in the details when it comes to dealing with the things men build.

—Sharon Lee and Steve Miller
The Cat Farm and Confusion Factory
Central Maine
August 21, 2013

———————

"Proud Robot," Henry Kuttner

Landed Alien

Pool Pilot and Tech Kara ven'Arith sat in the Station Master's office, on an uncomfortable, and cold, steel chair.

She sat alone, hands folded tightly in her lap, face under rigid control. Waiting...

A man was dead. A *pilot* was dead.

By her hand.

She turned her head to the left, and stared for a long moment at the door to the outer hallway and the rest of Codrescu Station. She turned her head to the right, and gave the door to the Station Master's inner office similar close study. Neither door was locked. Why would they be?

There was no place to go, and nothing, really, for her to do.

Save wait.

Wait on the verdict of those now discussing her and her actions, there in the inner office. Would she live? Would she die? Would she be banished to the planet's surface, to take her chances there?

They would decide: the Station Master, the Guild Master, her immediate supervisor, the head Tugwhomper, and the associate supervisor of the pilot pool.

Kara took a deep breath, and wished they would decide *soon*.

* * *

It was silent in the common room as the graduation list scrolled across the community screen. They were all seniors in this dorm; and

3

each a deal more solemn than even the suspense of the scrolling list might account for.

At the back of the room, Kara ven'Arith stood alone, and hopefully out of the eye of the dorm's loyalty monitor. *That* one had been dogging her steps for the last semester, trying to catch her in a "subversive" act. The monitor had been at great pains to explain Kara's precarious situation to her—the lack of three black marks was all that stood between Kara and the fate of her *very good friend*, Expelled Student Waitley.

The monitor had stared at her in what Kara supposed was intended to be a sad-but-stern manner, and which had been so ludicrous that she had been hard-put not to giggle. Worse, the thought of what Theo might say upon hearing her new title of honor was almost enough to send her into whoops.

It being fairly certain that she would earn one, if not two, of those missing black marks immediately for a failure to show proper respect, Kara had bitten the inside of her cheek and bowed her head, striving to give the impression of one too cowed by authority to speak.

The monitor *hrummphed*.

"You'd do better to sit up and meet my eye," she had snapped. "Sneaking alien ways won't improve your record."

Well, and that *had* almost brought her to join Theo. Kara had taken a deep breath, and lifted her head deliberately to meet the other woman's eyes.

"I am not an alien," she said calmly, in the Eylot dialect of Terran. "My family has held land on this planet for ninety-eight Standards."

The monitor, whose name was Peline Graf, frowned.

"And you think that makes you Eylotian?" she asked.

It was on the edge of Kara's tongue to say that she had been born on Eylot—but, after all, that did <u>not</u> make her Eylotian—even her delm taught so. They of Clan Menlark were <u>Liaden</u>, though based upon Eylot.

"You're nothing but a landed alien," Monitor Graf added, in a tone that made plain that she found this Eylotian legal reality not in the least amusing.

Kara folded her lips together and held the monitor's gaze until the other woman waved her hand in abrupt dismissal.

"I'm required to warn students who are in danger of expulsion. This has been your warning, ven'Arith. Watch yourself."

It had been, Kara had admitted to herself, after a long walk, a long shower, and a long, sleepless night, a fair warning, of its kind, and worth taking to heart. She had so much hanging, as the Terran phrase went, in Balance. Very nearly a Liaden meaning to Balance, there.

Well. She had seen what had happened to Theo, who had committed the dual crimes of not being Eylotian, and excelling beyond those who were. For those crimes, she had been targeted, trapped, and expelled. She, Kara ven'Arith, was the designated instrument of Theo's will in *that* matter. As such, she was honor-bound to keep all and any doors open through which Balance might enter.

That—and there was her family to consider. To be expelled so near to the completion of her course and flight-work, even if she could show political malice as the cause? That would scarcely please her mother or her delm. Indeed, it was very likely that she would be roundly scolded for having been so maladroit as to allow her enemies to prevail against her. Clan Menlark had not prospered as pilots and as mechanics on a culturally diverse world known for its effervescent politics because its children were either maladroit or stupid.

All that being so, she had watched herself, and also, with a sort of black humor, watched those who watched her. She held herself aloof from any ties of friendship, that she might not be tainted by anothers error; she studied; she flew; she tutored; she slept; and ate; and attended all and every politically significant rally and workshop offered on campus.

By doing these things, she insured her graduation, pilot's license in hand, as her mother and her delm expected.

Her mother next expected her to offer herself for hire as a pilot, that being the clan's main livelihood. There, duty. . .diverged. Kara's heart had long been with the clan's secondary business. Even as a child, she had dogged Uncle Bon Sel's every step in the repair shop, until in self-defense he gave her a wrench and taught her how to use it. Her determination was to continue in that line, now that she had done as her delm and her mother had commanded.

That being so, she filed her app with Howsenda Hugglelans, where she had a good multi-season record as a temp worker, and excellent relations with her supervisors, and with Aito, the Hugglelans Third Son. It was not at all unreasonable to think that she might be hired there as a mechanic or a tech, and best to have all her cards in hand before she brought the matter to her mother.

The application had not yet gained a reply, but here—here came the approach to her name on the screen. She straightened, waiting, hardly daring to breathe. What if something had happened? What if someone in Admin had decided to withhold her last grade points? What if she *had* been given a black mark, despite all her care? What if there was some new reg, put into place secretly, that had to do only with those who weren't "truly Eylotian"? It had happened before. . .

Her chest was tight. Surely the feed had slowed? But no, that was foolish, and there! Her name!

And next to her name, her standing in the class—low, but she had expected that—and at the end of the line, her license certification. . .

Candidate Second. . .

"Candidate Second?" she gasped, stunned. She had *earned* a firm second class license. She had the hours, she had passed the tests, she—

"Something wrong, ven'Arith?" asked Droy Petris, with false concern. Droy Petris watched her, also, though less diligently than the monitor.

She had spoken out loud, Kara thought. *Stupid*, to let caution go *now*. Still, there was a recover to hand.

"I was astonished," she said, truthfully; "I had no idea I'd graduate at such a level."

He looked at her suspiciously, and Loyalty Monitor Graf was seen to frown, but there wasn't a regulation forbidding a pilot to express surprise.

She hoped.

#

The fiveday between the end of class and the senior graduation ceremony was traditionally a festive time, featuring parties, and picnics, dances, and epic games of bowli bowl. It was a time when friendships were reaffirmed; when new addresses and mail drop codes were exchanged.

Kara, who deliberately had no friends, dutifully attended the meetings mandated by Admin. As she was a past-champion, she also took part in the bowli ball tournament where she reveled in the play until, in the quarter finals, her lack of current connections made it easy for her to be ganged up on and evicted early from the game.

Not wishing to risk any unpleasantness in the stands, she avoided spectating. Instead, she volunteer to polish one of the long-wing training sailplanes, that it would be a welcome meeting for its next pilot, and thus received the benefit of exercise.

She also took long, solitary walks around campus, carefully avoiding such places as might call unwanted attention to her, such as Belgraid dorm, which had once housed the Culture Club, since "discovered" to be a hotbed of subversive activity, designed to indoctrinate the unwary into the customs and lifestyles of planets that were not Eylot.

She returned to the dorm from one particularly long walk to find herself the sole occupant. That would have been more pleasing if she didn't suspect that Monitor Graf had planted spy-eyes about, to watch when she could not.

Still, the absence of her dorm-mates did give pleasure. Kara stopped to withdraw a fruit drink from the cold-box, and went to her room, shaking the bulb absently.

She closed the door—senior privilege—and sat down at her desk, bringing the computer live with a light touch, snapping the bulb open while she waited for her mail to download.

Three letters came in-queue. Kara ran her eye down the list as she sipped her drink.

The first letter was from Hugglelans. She opened it, bottom lip caught in her teeth. If she had an offer, or perhaps an invitation to interview. . .

But no.

Dear Applicant.

This letter is to inform you that your application for employment has been received. We regret to inform you that Howsenda Hugglelans is not hiring at this time.

Thank you for your interest, and the best of luck in your search for employment.

Human Resources Form Number 3

Kara stared at this missive for much longer than required to master its contents. *Not hiring?* she thought. *Or not hiring Liadens?*

The thought made her angry—and then frightened. If *Hugglelans* had bowed to the rising tide of politics. . .

She took a breath, filed the form, and looked to the next item in queue.

It was from the Dean of Students office. Her stomach clenched, and her mouth felt dry, despite the juice. She put the pod down on the edge of her desk, and opened the letter.

TO: Kara ven'Arith, Candidate Pilot Second Class

FROM: Anlingdin Pilot Certification Office

Candidate pilots are required to attend a re-orientation session immediately following graduation. At the conclusion of this session, those qualifying will see the candidate status removed and their license properly registered by the Eylot Pilots Guild.

Please report to Gunter Recreation Area on. . .

Kara squeezed her eyes shut, and mentally reviewed an exercise designed to restore clarity to a pilot's tired mind. That done, she took six deep, calming breaths before opening her eyes again and re-addressing the letter.

Her hands were cold and she was shaking, just a little, though that was anger, because they had found a way to hold her license hostage still longer! She had *earned* her Second Class license! Earned it! And now, she was being required to complete some other requirement—a requirement, she was certain was in place only for those who were not *truly Eylotian*! And what chance had she to qualify, to see her license properly recorded at the end of it all?

"Wait," she told herself, closing her eyes again. "Wait. Think."

She accessed another mental exercise, this to impose calm; then she did, indeed, think.

She had come this far. She had completed her coursework, gained her second class license, despite the oppressive oversight that had caused others of her classmates—friends from the Culture Club, and various others who had come from outworlds—to drop out and return home. Kara ven'Arith hadn't quit. She had been clever, she had kept her head down, she had kept herself informed of the changing requirements, and she had graduated.

She had done what was needed, and she could—she *would*—do whatever was necessary to clear this new barrier to claiming that which she had earned.

When she opened her eyes this time, her feelings were firmer, though they suffered a ripple when she saw that the re-orientation "session" was indeed a planetary month long.

And Gunter Recreation Area. . .was a wilderness campground, without even an air-breather landing field.

Her stomach clenched again, and she hurriedly closed the letter, marking it for later review, and opened the last file in the queue.

It was a personal note from Flight Instructor Orn Ald yos'Senchul, her academic adviser, inviting her to take tea with him—in an hour.

Kara smiled with real pleasure. Pilot yos'Senchul had been a support and a comfort, subtle as he was. He remained at Anlingdon, so he had told her, in honor of his contract, which the new administra-

tion was unexpectedly too canny to cancel out of hand, having perhaps learned a lesson from the Slipper instructor's dismissal.

But—good gods, the time! Kara leapt to her feet and ran for the
shower.

#

"A tenday tour?" Kara took the paper Pilot yos'Senchul held out
to her across the tea-table, and sat somewhat ill-at-ease, cup in one
hand, folded printout in the other.

"Please," her host murmured, "take a moment to familiarize yourself. I thought first of you when I read it, and I am curious to know if
you feel the same."

*Immediate need. Codrescu Station, Eylot Nearspace. Student me-
chanic to tour, inspect, and repair station systems under supervision of
Master Mechanic. Long hours. Union rates. Teacher recommendation
or references required. First qualified hired.*

Kara felt her pulse quicken. It wasn't a full-time job at Hugglelans, but it was far better than a walk in vacuum without a spacesuit.

She frowned, calculating. The graduation ceremony was in three
days—an empty formality since her mother had let her know that
circumstances would unfortunately keep her kin from making the trip
to Anlingdin.

"I have my ratings and references from my break-work at Hugglelans," she said, speaking aloud, but more to herself than to Pilot
yos'Senchul. "A tenday tour. . ." She frowned at the print-out again.
"*Immediate need*," she mused, and looked up to find his gaze very at-
tentive on her face.

"If *immediate* means that I may start within the next two local days," she said slowly, "I can do the tour and return in good time to attend the re-orientation class."

"Do you mean to do so?" Pilot yos'Senchul asked.

She looked at him in surprise.

"Well, I *must*, if ever I want to free my license of that wretched notation of *candidate*!"

"Yes, of course," he said, and used his chin to point at the paper she still held. "Do I hear that you are interested in filling that position, assuming that *immediately* is found to be accommodating?"

"I am, yes."

"Very good." He put his cup down and stood, slipping the paper away from her with his natural hand while the fingers of his prosthetic spelled out, *rise! quick lift!*

Startled, she came to her feet. "Sir?"

"Go quickly and pack. If I may—pack heavy, lest there is a dorm cleaning while you are away. I will meet you at the shuttle in an hour."

"Sir, but—"

"I had said that I thought first of you. Having done so, I sent the master mechanic my recommendation, forwarding your references from Hugglelans, which were available to me, as your adviser. He replied that he would have you, if you were interested. We have established that you are interested. And I should tell you that *immediately* in this instance means, according to Master Thelly, *three days or a week ago*."

"But, I—"

"You may send an introduction from the shuttle," he interrupted. "Or perhaps you've changed your mind, and that is why you stand here when your ship needs you?"

"*No*, sir!" She cried, and bowed—respect to an instructor.

Then, she ran.

#

Kara's personal effects, with those things that Theo had entrusted to her, were in the shuttle's modest holding area. She was in the pilot's chair, Pilot yos'Senchul sitting second. Once they had broken orbit, she had 'beamed a message to Master Mechanic Thelly, introducing herself and informing him that she was on her way to take up duty.

She was doing the set-up for Codrescu approach when the master's reply arrived, telling her to find him in Sub-sector Blue Eleven's machine room after she'd been cleared through.

"I'm going to have to hit the deck running," she commented, not unpleased by the prospect of getting right to work.

"Union rates," her co-pilot murmured. "Be certain to keep track of your hours; Master Thelly is quite capable of working three shifts in four, and he expects his assistants to do as much."

She shot a glance at him, but only saw the side of his face, calm as it usually was, his eyes on his screens.

"That sounds like the voice of experience," she said. "Did you 'prentice with Master Thelly, Pilot?"

"In fact, I did, some few years ago. He was at first. . .doubtful. . .regarding the utility to himself of a one-armed assistant. I was able to put those doubts to rest, and learned a good deal in Balance." He glanced at her.

"You will find the master a thorough teacher."

"Good," said Kara.

The board pinged for her attention, then, and she gave it.

#

"This way, Pilot," yos'Senchul said, waving her into a dim side passage that was definitely not the route to the Station Master's office.

"Master Thelly..." she began.

"Master Thelly will still have work for you in half-an-hour," he said.

Kara sighed and followed him, the peculiar taste of station air on her tongue. She had been to Codrescu Station a dozen times or more, and thought she knew its maze of corridors pretty well. This hall, so thin that she and Pilot yos'Senchul—both comfortably Liaden-sized—needed to proceed in single-file, wasn't at all familiar. It was a utility hall, she thought, noting the access panels set high and low. Well, perhaps it would soon become familiar.

Ahead, their hall ended in another—and this one Kara did recall.

"The Guild Office?" she asked.

"Indeed," he answered. Before them was the door, and a guard beside it, sidearm holstered.

"yos'Senchul and ven'Arith, to see the Guild Master," her companion said. "We are, I think, expected."

"You're on the list, pilots," the guard confirmed, opening the door for them. "Straight ahead."

#

Guild Master Peltzer ran her card, made a noise strongly reminiscent of a snort, and nodded in her direction.

"Be a couple minutes to review your files, Pilot. You wanna make yourself comfortable here? I got a feeling Pilot yos'Senchul wants to have a private word with me. Is that right, Orn Ald?"

Pilot yos'Senchul inclined his head gravely. "You know me too well."

"Just about well enough, I'm thinking. Step into my office. Pilot, please, take some rest."

The two men stepped in to the Guild Master's inner office and the door closed. Kara, too energized to sit, *or* to be comfortable, walked quietly to the small green garden across from the intake desk, its tall fronds waving in the breeze from an air duct. An agreeable gurgle of running water came from somewhere in the depths of the tiny jungle.

Kara knelt down and considered the greenery. There were, as she knew from previous visits, norbears living among the fronds—one quite old, and the other quite young. She would, she thought, like to have the attention of a norbear at the moment, though it would be rude to wake them, or to disturb their pretty habitat.

She was about to rise again, when the fronds dipped more deeply than could be accounted for by the small breeze, and here came the elder norbear—rust colored and thin of fur—marching deliberately forward, through the fronds and out of the garden entirely, climbing familiarly onto Kara's knee.

"Hevelin, good-day to you," she said, stroking his head gently. He burbled and pushed into her fingers, demanding a more vigorous scrubbling.

Kara smiled and settled cross-legged to the floor, careful of the old norbear's balance, and rubbed his head with vigor. His pleased burbling seem to leach her restlessness, and she sighed, half-closing her eyes.

An image came into her head, lazily, like a dream—an image she recognized as Pilot yos'Senchul. She recalled him entering the Guild Master's office, and the image faded, to be replaced by the impression of a pointed, pale face dominated by fierce dark eyes, framed by blow-away pale hair that Kara knew to be as soft and warm as feathers.

"No," she murmured. "Theo's not with me, though I have her things. I'm here for a tenday tour, to assist Master Thelly."

A man's round, red-cheeked face faded through Theo's, his eyes blue and sharp, the lines around them made by worry, laughter—or by both. Master Thelly, perhaps.

She felt herself sinking into a languor; almost, she felt she could have a nap.

Happily for her dignity, the door behind her opened at that moment. The languor fled, leaving behind a feeling of tingling alertness. She opened her eyes to look up, at Orn Ald yos'Senchul, and, further up, at Guild Master Peltzer.

"Hevelin took the edge off, did he?" he said with a nod. "Worth a full night's sleep, one of Hevelin's purr-breaks. If you'll stand up, Pilot, we can get your little matter finished up and send you to the Station Master for registration."

"Thank you," Kara said to Hevelin. "Would you like to go back to the garden?"

It appeared that Hevelin did not. He clambered up her arm to her shoulder and grabbed onto her collar to steady himself.

"I'd say that's plain," said Guild Master Peltzer, moving over to the intake desk. Kara came to her feet, careful of her passenger, and stepped up.

"All right now. Pilot. This'll take a bit to propagate across the databases, so I'll just drop a note to the Station Master and to Master Thelly, letting them know the news." He tapped keys, and Kara, Hevelin humming in her ear, waited with what patience she could muster for someone to tell *her* the news.

"Right, then. Here you are, Pilot." He held her license out in her general direction, while his other hand and his eyes were still on the computer.

Kara took the card, Hevelin all but deafening her with his purr, and slipped it away into an inner pocket.

"Sir?" she said. "May I –"

He looked up, catching her gaze with his, and inclined his head formally.

"Congratulations, Second Class pilot Kara ven'Arith."

She stiffened. "Your pardon, Guild Master. I am, I believe, *Candidate* Second Class Pilot ven'Arith."

He shook his head, his smile tight.

"That's according to the so-called Pilots Guild of Eylot, which has no standing with the Interstellar Starship Pilots Guild. Eylot Guild can deny our licenses and our regs 'til they're short of air, but at the end of the shift, they're a local independent piloting group. Anybody lifting with an Eylot Guild ticket is just another indie flyer, far as *this* Guild is concerned."

Hevelin's purring hit an ecstatic crescendo.

Kara looked closely at the Guild Master's grim face. She transferred her gaze to Pilot yos'Senchul, who inclined his head gravely, and murmured, "A signal achievement, Pilot. Well done."

"You brought me here for this, didn't you?" she demanded.

"In part," he allowed, with a slight smile. "I did also think of you first when the tenday tour came into my queue."

Kara took a breath. "Pilot yos'Senchul," she began – and stopped as he held up his hand.

"Please, honor me with the use of my given name, now that we are colleagues – and comrades."

She frowned at him. Colleagues, yes, because they were now both certified by the same guild, though he was Master to her Second Class. Comrade, though...

"Do you have work on-station? But your contract at the Academy—"

"The present administration has placed conditions upon my continued employment which I cannot in conscience accept. Therefore, I have offered myself to Guild Master Peltzer, who believes he may be able to find a use for me."

The Guild Master laughed.

"More like sixteen uses for you!" he said. "I figure to whittle it down to three, after I talk with people."

"The Academy's shuttle. . ." Kara protested, thinking of *Cherpa* in Berth Fourteen.

"I will send the key down on the station shuttle. Whomever the Academy chooses to take it down may ride the jump seat on the supply wagon."

"Details," pronounced the Guild Master, waving a bluff hand. "What the two of you need to do is get registered with the Station Master office. Soon's that's done, we can start getting some work out of you!"

"Indeed," said Pilot yos'Senchul, with a slight, comradely bow. "After you, Kara."

"Yes," she said, and turned to put Hevelin back among the greenery.

#

The Pilot handling her forms for the Station Master was called Fortch; his work blouse was that of a commercial transfer company.

He looked her up and down before she announced herself, and then with a spark of interest when she did.

"ven'Arith, eh? I gather you've been expected for a day or so. Forms have been waiting – fill and sign and. . ."

Seeing her glance at his name and the Certified Pilot logo on his breast pocket, he nodded and tapped it with one finger.

"Company gave me my uniform the day the newest rules came down," he told her as he checked her work. "All I needed was the paper. But you know what's happening, and I do: they say I'm no pilot until I get *their* paper. Can't get *their* paper 'cause my father's brother was suspected of being on the wrong side twenty years ago. I get to do some tugwork here, they put me in the pool. I help out here on the slow days." He sighed, glancing at the form screen. "At least you'll get a chance to pick yours up."

Kara nodded. Tugwork meant he was likely a third class, maybe an air pilot too – and that was hard. If his family went back for generations and was thought unreliable, he might never get work on-world.

There was a small chirp and he started nervously; and out of the air the order "Send in the new one, Fortch! Master Thelly's in a snit to get her on the job!"

The aide jerked his head at the inner door, and handed the forms back to her.

"Luck. Hope to catch you around."

#

She'd worked overshift – not unusual, and becoming more usual as she double-timed herself – working two full shifts, then cramming a class into her so-called rec shift. The class she was currently embroiled in, remote repair, required not only coursework, but board time, not with a sim, but with an actual remote, out on Codrescu's skin. Time and necessity being what they were, she had to grab her practice sessions betwixt and between. The work shifts today had gone long, whereby she had been late to log into class, and so last to take the remote.

The work had not been mere practice, but real work, resetting a trio of lock-anchors on Ten Rod Two, the arm that the Guild supply ship *Zircon Sea* was due to use. With the strangenesses attendant to Eylot's politics the *Sea's* technical and parts refills were much needed to make up for several quarters worth of back-orders, missing items, and out-and-out damaged-on-receipt goods. Given the state of supplies, she'd triple checked her work, and delayed herself more. . .

And now, she was *starving*.

At least there was an easy answer to that; very possibly the first easy answer she had been confronted with today.

She turned down the hall to the Hub Caf, ran her station card under the reader and picked up a tray.

Quickly, she onloaded soy soup, fresh salad, and a more-or-less fresh-baked roll, and a cup of lemon-water. She turned from the serving bar, expecting at this shift and hour to have her choice of tables – which wasn't. . .quite true.

There was only one other diner in the Caf – a man in coveralls much like those she wore. Uncharacteristically, his shoulders were hunched, his arms crossed on the table before him, his attention wholly on the screen before him.

Kara hesitated, took a breath and went forward. Comrades held duty to the well-being of each other; and even if they had not been comrades, she owed him the same sort of care he had shown for her.

"Orn Ald? May I join you?"

He looked up, and even in the dim lighting, she could see that his cheeks were wet.

For a Liaden to so far forget *melant'i* as to weep in public – that was appalling. That *Orn Ald yos'Senchul* should do so could signal nothing less than a cataclysm.

Kara clattered her tray to the table, staring at him.

"*What has happened?*"

For answer, he spun the screen.

She recognized the *Eylot Gazette*, the Liaden community's social newspaper, open to the death notices.

There was only one.

Lef Nal vin'Eved Clan Selbry, of injuries sustained during Anlingdin Academy Graduate Re-orientation camp. Selbry Herself stands as the instrument of his will. Clan and kin grieve.

Kara remembered him only vaguely – they had been in few classes together and he hadn't been a bowli ball player. He had, in fact, been rather frail, all the moreso for a certain single-mindedness that allowed him to discount every obstacle between himself and a goal. Lef Nal was, thought Kara, easily the sort of person who might fall off a cliff by reason of having momentarily forgotten about the effects of gravity.

She raised her eyes to Orn Ald's ravaged face.

He had, she saw in relief, used a napkin to dry his cheeks, but not even Liaden social training could hide the desolation in his eyes.

"I have also had a private letter on the topic," he said quietly. "It would appear that Pilot vin'Eved has been reft from clan and kin as a result of what is termed a *hazing*. He and several others had been identified as lacking a proper reverence for the new political scenery, and so were placed in. . .special circumstances, in order to cow them.

The others are injured, but will survive." He sighed, and spun the screen to face him again.

"One save a year," he murmured, and she looked at him sharply.

"What is that?"

"Ah." He raised his eyes to hers, his mouth twisting. "When I was newcome to Anlingdin Academy, the elder instructor who was assigned as my mentor taught that we who teach must sometimes rescue our students – from themselves, from bad advice, from the expectations of kin, or of the world. She had it, as a point of philosophy—or perhaps of honor—that *one save a year made all the rest worthwhile.*"

Kara slid onto the stool across from him, pushing her tray with the cooling soup and wilting salad to one side.

"You saved me," she said, very softly; and then, whispering, because even the thought was too terrible to bear.

"Was it only *us* – the landed aliens – who were given conditional licenses, Orn Ald?"

He shook his head. "A few less than half, by my count, were in your case, and in. . .Pilot vin'Eved's case. A handful of outworld students received conditional licenses, also, but they were merely required to certify that they would be leaving the planet after graduation."

It was easier to breathe. She sighed, slipped off of the stool and bowed as one who was cognizant of debt.

"Do not think of it," he murmured. "Our relative *melant'i* at the time placed one in the position of protector. Honor is fulfilled, on all sides, and Balance maintains." He shook his head, and said, in subdued Terran, "I advised him to go home and place it in the hands of his delm."

And Lef Nal had decided that school matters were the student's to solve, and matters of one's license best resolved by the pilot.

It was, Kara thought, precisely what she would have done.

Indeed, it was precisely what she *had* decided to do, until Orn Ald yos'Senchul had whisked her off for a tenday tour, and showed her a way to gain her license without condition.

When the fill-in assignment had come open, near the end of her tenday, she had contacted her mother and her delm, who had advised her, in their separate faces, to pursue opportunity at the station. Her mother had said that their own small yard was for the moment empty and thus closed, for want of business. Her delm had noted that all Menlark pilots were for the present pursuing hire contracts outworld, and that none were expected to return to Eylot in the foreseeable future.

Failing an outworld piloting contract, Codrescu Station was, said her mother, the best place for her.

She looked again to Orn Ald. As the one owed, it was his to assert what might be the cost, or if they resided in Balance. A comfort, certainly, but rather chilly. A comrade might offer more warmth.

Kara inclined her head.

"Forgive that I notice your distress. I merely do so that I may offer relief, if it is desired."

His eyebrows rose, and she braced herself for a light comment regarding their relative ages. But, when it came his response was only a mannerly, "The offer is gently made. However, I fear I would bring little to the cause of comfort – and you are wanted in not too many hours at your duty."

He slid off his stool and bowed to her as between comrades, indeed.

"I will leave you to your meal. Speaking with you has been a balm. Good-shift, Kara."

"Good shift, Orn Ald," she answered, and turned to watch him walk away before once again taking a stool and pulling her meal toward her.

After a moment, she stood again, picked up the tray and carried it over to the disposal.

#

The bowli ball zagged, then zagged again, avoiding Bilton's grasp as adroitly as if it had eyes and reason. Kara, next nearest, jumped, spinning lightly, and capturing the ball against her chest. It kicked, not hard, and the moment her feet hit decking, she threw it well to the left of Yangi.

The rangy red-haired pilot showed her teeth in what might equally have been a savage smile or a grimace of pain, and launched into a long vertical lunge. She snatched the ball, holding it in the crook of her elbow as she tucked to roll mid-air, coming down flat-footed, knees bent. Her smile grew positively feral as she threw ball with considerable strength, straight down at the decking.

Predictably—at least to those wise in the ways of the device and the game—the ball shot upward. Unpredictably, it skated to the right, into the space occupied by the hapless Fortch, the least apt of their players, nearly as new on station as she, and yet unaccustomed to his local mass.

He jumped for the ball, twisting in an effort to eat his unwanted momentum, actually got a hand on—

"Kara ven'Arith!" The all-call rattled the walls of the so-called Arena.

Bilton leapt, and came spinning to the deck, the bowli ball dancing along his fingers, shedding energy as it did.

Yangi grabbed Fortch by the belt just in time to keep him from ramming his nose against the wall.

Kara, flatfoot and hands at her side, stood waiting.

"Kara ven'Arith to Central Repair," Master Thelly's voice blared. "Kara ven'Arith to Central Repair, *now*!"

#

"Sorry 'bout it, Kara—know it's your rec shift. Vechi had an accident in Green-Mid-Six. Got 'er out to the clinic, but the work'd just got started, and needs to be finished. You got least hours on the card."

"So I win," she said, showing cheerful in the face of his worry, though she was worried, too. This accident was the fifth among the tech-crew in the last eighteen Station-days; more than the total accidents for the last six Standard months. Not only newbies, either—two old hands had spent a couple work shifts each in the station's autodoc, getting patched up from injuries from 'freak accidents'.

Kara finished belting on her kit, and looked 'round.

"Vechi's wagon's still down in Mid-Six," Master Thelly said. "Had to carry her out."

Kara stared at him.

"What happened this time?"

"Wild charge," Master Thelly said, looking even more worried. "You be careful, hear me?"

"I'm always careful," Kara told him, picking up her tea bottle.

He grunted. "So's Vechi."

#

Green-Mid-Six was a well-lit and roomy utility hall in a low-grav segment of the station. Kara had helped with the complete maintenance overhaul of the systems housed in this hall during her tenday tour. Vechi's orders, still up on the work wagon's screen, were to check an anomaly in Bay Four. The hatch was off, and leaning neatly against the wall. The test leads were still tidily wrapped on the wagon, so the wild charge must have struck Vechi either as she removed the hatch, or when she did her first eye-scan. That was standard procedure for a tech with an anomaly report to retire: A visual scan to make sure there wasn't any obvious damage—melted leads, snapped fuses, anything broken or compromised.

If the tech's eyeballs or nose didn't locate a problem, then the leads from the wagon were attached, and a series of diagnostics were run.

A wild charge build-up, thought Kara, pulling on her gloves, while contemplating the open access from the side of the wagon—that would create an anomaly, all right.

It would also create damage with a very particular signature. Once identified, all that remained was for the tech to pinpoint the cause, for the reports, and file a work order for rebuild.

Gloves on and light in hand, Kara advanced on the open access port.

Even though she knew what she'd see, Kara still blinked as her light illuminated the interior of the hatch.

Carnage was the word that came to her mind; and also the thought that there would be no identifying the failed source; there simply wasn't enough left to support a forensic diagnostic. The smell of ozone was not completely gone, nor that of the antiseptic sprays they'd used on Vechi.

She returned to the wagon, tapped up the main schematic screen and traced the power flow.

The station operated with tertiary back-ups, only sensible in so vulnerable a habitat as a space station. She was pleased to see that the back-up had come online without a glitch and there had been no discernible disruption of service.

So much was to the good. She opened another screen, logged the damage and created the work order for the rebuild. In plain truth, she was likely to draw that one, but right now she was Vechi, with Vechi's orders to clear.

She tapped the screen, bringing up the list of work orders. Anomaly resolution went to the top of a given roster-list, so this had been Vechi's first stop on her shift. It glowed yellow on the screen—begun, but not logged as complete.

Below was a long list of work orders, all patiently showing green—waiting for tech.

Kara sipped from her tea-bottle as she created a ref-file, attached the open, incomplete, order to the rebuild order, raised her finger to tap the next task in line—and stopped, frowning.

Vechi was the fifth tech injured in the line of duty. Had the others all been checking anomalies, too?

In less than thirty seconds, she had the anomalies report open on one side of the wagon's screen; on the other, the tech department's injury report.

The injured techs: Vechi, Mardin, Whistler, Harfer, and Gen Arb—and yes, each had been checking an anomaly report when they had been injured.

Kara's fingers were quicker than her thoughts. She called up the real-time functions, using her key for the big ops board, that she sat on rotation every eight station-days.

The wagon's screen was too small to accommodate the whole function screen, but all Kara wanted to do was to set an alarm. That done, she opened up the next work order in-queue.

#

About half-way through Vechi's shift, Kara paused between jobs to file a manual schedule adjustment. There was, she reasoned, no sense going off duty for one shift, only to have to report back for her regular work-shift. Best to just keep on, with the loan of Vechi's wagon, and swap out her second shift for rest. That would get her two rest shifts in a row, and put her back onto her regular schedule.

The system OK'd the change, which meant that Master Thelly was on maintenance himself, and would scold her the next time they met, per standard procedure.

Content with her changes, Kara finished out Vechi's shift, closed the list of completed work orders, signed in as herself and downloaded her own run of work.

She was in Green-Mid-Forty-Five; her work started in Blue-Mid-Twelve, conveniently near. Kara regarded the change of venue as a break.

She sipped tea as she walked, the wagon following. The best route to Blue-Mid-Twelve involved a shortcut through Orange, where the root of Ten Rod Two joined the station structure proper.

And there she quite unexpectedly found Fortch, the pool pilot who had not yet mastered the station's gravity, in front of the utility-core for the arm, an access hatch wide open, and several tools haphazardly sticking from his pockets and belt.

"What are you doing in the tech-tunnels, Pilot?" she asked, using her tea-bottle as a pointer, her voice sharper than it ought to be, for truly, he could be temp-help, or—

But if he was temp-help, where was his repair wagon? Where was his kit?

Fortch seemed to feel himself at a disadvantage. He licked his lips.

"Kara! I didn't know you were working down here!"

"And I didn't you were working down here."

"Oh, well I am – working. Filling in. Just checking something out for Master Thelly, that's all. There was a glitch on the screen and he asked me to – but wait, I need to talk to you about your license problem..."

He was moving, as if trying to stay between her and the open hatch. Lights were on, and covers hinged back from equipment.

Behind her, the anomaly alarm went off on the work wagon, and three things happened in a quick succession.

Fortch jumped toward her, a spanner suddenly in his hand.

Kara spun as if she were playing bowli ball, ducked under his outstretched arms, using the open tea-bottle to fend off the tool he swung down. There was a clang, the bottle was torn from her hand and spun away, splashing tea everywhere. Her spin continued as his lunge faltered; she came up behind—and pushed him away from her, hard as she could, toward the open utility room.

He, inept in the station environment, skidded on the tea-splashed deck, arms pinwheeling now, half-fell and half slid, snatched for his balance, cursing —and lost his balance altogether, striking his shoulder on the access door and crashing heavily into the room, arm up in a desperate and failing bid not to fall into the panels and wiring.

There was a sharp snap and a dazzling flash, and he collapsed to the decking, unmoving.

#

The door to the Station Master private office opened, and Kara stood up, preferring to meet her fate thus.

"Tech ven'Arith, thank you for your patience," the Station Master said gently, giving her a bow as well-meaning as it was meaningless. "You're free to go."

She blinked at him.

"To go?" she repeated. "Go—where?"

"To your conapt, I'd say," Master Thelly stuck in. "You got the next three shifts off—use 'em to sleep!"

"But—" She looked among them until she found Orn Ald yos'Senchul's face. "Fortch is dead."

"So he is, and that is unfortunate, since there were questions that various of us would have liked to ask him. Clearly, however, he was undertaking sabotage against the station and his efforts might have killed hundreds. Stopping him was of utmost importance—and stop him you did." He inclined his head.

Kara noticed that her hands were clenched. She opened them, and shook her fingers out.

"But—why?" she asked. "Why was he trying to. . .harm the station?"

Bringo, the Chief Tugwhomper, looked grave.

"Had a drink wit' the boy not so long ago," he said slowly. "Shortenin' it considerable, he told me he figured out how to get his paper, Eylot-side."

Kara shivered, suddenly cold.

"By killing the station?"

"Now, missy. Coulda just drunk too much coil fluid and talkin' big. Cheer 'imself up, like."

"There will be an investigation," said the Station Master. "Might be something in his quarters will be helpful. In the meanwhile, Pilot ven'Arith, the lesson you're to take away from you is that you acted in self-defense – properly acted in self defense. If Fortch hadn't had the main power bus to the arm open he'd be alive. I'd say the fatal mistake was his, not yours."

Orn Ald's voice then, quick, comforting Liaden preceding a gentle bow between comrades.

"The station is in your debt, Kara."

"That's right, and we don't aim to stay that way," said Guild Master Peltzer. "There's a reward for preserving environmental integrity. Understand, it's not what any of us can call exact Balance—more like a symbolic Balance. Be as may, I reckon that reward's gonna show up in your account." He gave the Station Master a hard look, and that individual smiled.

"Without a doubt, Guild Master. Without a doubt."

"That's all set now," said Master Thelly, firmly. "Kara—go get some rest."

"Yes," she said, numb, but with a dawning sense of relief. She bowed a simple bow of respect to the group of them, and turned toward the door.

As she stepped into the hall, she found Orn Ald yos'Senchul next to her.

"Will you share a meal with me, comrade, and allow me escort you to your conapt?"

"Yes," she said again, and considered him. "And you will tell me everything that the others didn't want to tell me, won't you Orn Ald?"

"Oh, yes," he said serenely. "I'll do that."

Eleutherios

It had been many years since the organ had last given voice. Friar Julian had been a younger man—though by no means a *young* man—then, and had wept to hear the majesty brought forth by his fingers.

Godsmere Abbey had been great, then, before the punishments visited by earth and air. Now it, like the city surrounding, was. . .not quite a ruin. Just. . .very much less than it once had been.

Though it no longer worked, Friar Julian cared for the organ, still, waxing the wood, polishing the bright-work, dusting the keys, the bench, the pedals. As the organist, it had been his duty to care for the organ. Duty did not stop simply because the organ was broken.

Indeed, it was all of his duty, now: the care and keeping of odd objects—some whole, some broken, others too strange to know—and odd people in similar states of being. The odd people brought the odd objects, for the glory of the gods and their consorts, and the Abbey sheltered both, as best it might.

It seemed fitting.

Before the earthquake, before the Great Storm, Godsmere Abbey had the patronage of the wealthy, and the high. Witness the walls: titanium-laced granite that withstood the quake damage-free—saving some very small cracks and fissures; the roof-tiles which had denied wind and rain; the rows of carven couches in the nave—why, the organ itself!

They were gone now—the high, the wealthy, and the wise. Gone from the city of Collinswood, and from the planet of Fimbul, too;

gone to some other, less contentious place, where they might be comfortably safe.

In the meantime, there was no lack of work for those few friars who remained of the once-populous spiritual community of Godsmere. With loss and want, their tasks had become simpler—care for the sick, feed the hungry, nurture the feeble; and curate the collection of artifacts that filled the North Transept, and spilled into the South.

From time to time, the Abbey accepted boarders, though a far different class than had previously leased the courtyard-facing rooms, seeking tranquility in the simplicity of their surroundings, and the sloughing off, for a time, at least, the cares that weighed their spirits.

A bell rang, reverberating along the stone walls: the call to the mid-morning petition.

Friar Julian passed the dust cloth over the organ's face one more time before tucking the cloth into the organist's bench.

"I will come again," he promised it, softly, as he always did.

Then, he turned and hurried down the steps, out of the organ niche, to join his brothers in faith in giving thanks to the gods and their consorts for the dual gifts of life and conscience.

#

Later in the day, another bell rang, signaling a petitioner at the narthex. Friar Anton stood ostiary this day, and it was he who came to Friar Julian in the kitchen, to say that two city constables awaited him in the nave.

Friar Julian took off his apron, and nodded to Layman Voon, who was peeling vegetables.

"Please," he said, "call another to finish here for me. I may be some time, and the meal should not be delayed."

"Yes, Friar," Layman Voon said, and reached for the counter-side mic, to call for Layman Met, which was scarcely a surprise. Voon and Met had vowed themselves to each other in the eyes, and with the blessings of, the gods and their consorts, and worked together whenever it was possible.

Friar Julian and Friar Anton walked together along the back hallway.

"How many?" asked Friar Julian.

"One only," replied Anton.

That was mixed news. They had been without for some number of months, and while one was certainly better than none, two—or even four—would have been very welcome, indeed.

On the other hand, it was true that supplies were low in these weeks between the last planting and the first harvests, and one would put less strain upon them than four. Unless. . .

"In what state?" Friar Julian asked.

"Whole." Anton was a man of few words.

Friar Julian nodded, relieved that there would be no call upon their dangerously depleted medical supplies.

They came to the nave door. Anton passed on to his post at the narthex, and the great, formal entrance, while Julian opened an inner, passed through it into the clergy room, and thence, by another door, into the nave itself.

Three men stood in the central aisle, among the rows of gilt and scarlet couches. Two wore the dirt-resistant duty suits of the city constabulary. Out of courtesy, they had raised their visors, allowing Father Julian sight of two hard, lean faces that might have belonged to brothers.

The third man was shorter, stocky; dressed in the post-disaster motley of a city-dweller. His hair was black and unruly, his face round and brown. Black eyes snapped beneath fierce black eyebrows. An equally fierce, and shaggy, black mustache adorned his upper lip.

He held his arms awkwardly before him, crossed at the wrist. Friar Julian could see the sullen gleam of the binder beneath one frayed blue sleeve. He turned his head at Friar Julian's approach, and the cleric saw a line of dried blood on the man's neck.

"Just one today, Fadder," called the policeman on the prisoner's right. "He's a sly 'un, though."

Friar Julian stopped, and tucked his hands into the wide sleeves of his robe.

"Is he violent?" he asked, eying the man's sturdy build. "We are a house of peace."

"Violent? Not him! Caught 'im coming outta Trindle's Yard after hours, wida baga merch on his shoulder. Problem is, nuthin' caught 'im going in, and t'snoops was all up and workin'. 'Spector wants a vestigation, so you got a guest."

"There's something strange with his ID, too," said the other policeman, sternly. "Citizens Office is looking into that."

"But violent—nothin' like!" The first policeman took up the tale once more. "He ran, sure he did—who wouldn't? Nothin' to be ashamed of, us catching 'im. And he's smart, too—aincha?"

He dug an elbow into the prisoner's side. It might as well have been a breath of wind, for all the attention the man gave it. The policeman looked back to Friar Julian.

"We put the chip in, then stood back, like we do, so he could make a run fer it and get The Lesson. 'cept this guy, he don't run! Smart, see? We hadda walk away from 'im 'til he dropped off the meter and got the zap." He looked at the prisoner.

"Gotta have The Lesson, man. That's regs."

The prisoner stared at him, mouth hidden beneath his mustache.

"Not very talkative," the second policeman said, and opened one of his many belt pouches.

"The judge says board for two weeks," he said. "If the investigation goes longer, we'll re-up in two-week increments. If it goes shorter, the next boarder's fee will be pro-rated by the amount of overage."

Friar Julian slipped his hands out of his sleeves and stepped forward to pick the coins off of the gloved palm.

"Yes," he said calmly, fingers tight around the money, "that is the usual arrangement."

"Then we'll leave 'im to ya," the first policeman said. "Arms up, m'boy!"

That last was addressed to the prisoner, who raised his arms slightly, black eyes glittering.

The policeman unsnapped the binders while his partner walked across the nave to the safe. He used the special police-issue key to unlock it, and placed the small silver control box inside. Then he locked the safe, and sealed it.

He looked over his shoulder.

"Ponnor!" he called.

The prisoner pivoted smoothly to face him.

"You pay attention to this seal, now! It'll snap and blow if you try to get in here—that's the straight truth. The blast'll take your fingers, if it doesn't take your head. So, just sit tight, got it? The friar'll take good care of you."

"I have it," the man said, his voice low, and surprisingly lyrical.

"Right, then. We're gone. Good to see you again, Friar."

"May the gods and their consorts look with favor upon your efforts," Friar Julian said; seeing Friar Anton approaching from the direction of the North Transept. He had been listening, of course. The ostiary always listened, when there were policeman in the nave.

The policeman followed him out, leaving Friar Julian alone with the man named Ponnor.

* * *

The *garda* left them, escorted by the *gadje* who had admitted them to this place. Niku rubbed his right wrist meditatively, and considered the one who would *take good care of him*, Fadder Friar.

This *gadje* holy man was old, with a mane of white hair swept back from a formidable forehead. He had a good, strong nose, and a firm, square chin. Between chin and nose, like a kitten protected by wolves, were the soft lips of a child. White stubble glittered icily down his pale cheeks. His eyes were blue, and sad; far back, Niku perceived a shadow, which might be the remnants of his holiness, as shabby as his brown robe.

It was, Niku reflected, surprising that even a *gadje* holy man should accept the coin of the *garda*. Niku had no opinion of *gadje* in general, but his opinion of holiness had been fixed by the *luthia* herself. And among the blessed Bedel there was no one more blessed than the *luthia*, who cared for the body and soul of the *kompani*.

Well. The *luthia* was not with him, and he had more pressing concerns than the state of any single *gadje's* soul. It could be said that his present situation was dire—Niku himself would have said so, save for his faith in his brother Fada.

Still, a man needed to survive until Fada could come, so he looked to the holy *gadje*, produced a smile, and a little nod of the head.

"Sir," he said. *Gadje* liked to be called *sir*; it made them feel elevated above others. And the *garda* had shown scant reverence for this one's holiness.

The holy *gadje* returned both smile and nod.

"My name is Friar Julian," he said. "I am the oldest of the friars who remain at Godsmere, and it is my joyous burden to bring the prayers of the people to the attention of the gods and their consorts."

Niku, to whom this was so much nonsense, nonetheless smiled again, and nodded.

"Within these walls, my son, you are safe from error, for the gods do not allow a man to sin while he is in their keeping."

"It is well to be sinless," Niku said flippantly

It seemed to Niku that the holiness far back in Friar Julian's eyes burned bright for an instant, and he regretted his impertinence. Truly, the gods of this place had failed him, for it *was* a sin to mock a holy man, even a *gadje* holy man. The *luthia* would say, *especially* a *gadje* holy man, for *gadje* are so little blessed.

"Let me show you where you will sleep," said Friar Julian; "and introduce you to the others."

Niku froze. Others? *Others* might pose a problem, when Fada came.

"Other prisoners?" he asked.

Friar Julian frowned.

"You are our only boarder at present," he said stiffly. "The others to whom I would make you known are friars, as I am, and lay brothers. This we will do over the meal." He raised a hand and beckoned. "Come with me."

* * *

Ponnor walked the length of his room, placed a hand on the bed, opened the door to the 'fresher, closed it, opened and closed the closet door.

He turned, and asked, in his blunt way.

"What will be my occupation?"

Friar Julian was pleased. Despite his rough appearance, it would seem that this boarder had a sense of what was due a house of the gods. Most did not understood, and in fact, the agreement between Godsmere Abbey and the city constables stated that no boarder would be required to labor.

So it was that Friar Julian said, "You may do whatever you like."

Bright black eyes considered him from beneath lowering brows.

"If that is so, then I *would like* to return to my grandmother."

Friar Julian sighed, and held his hands out, palms up and empty, to signify his powerlessness.

"That," he admitted, "you may not do."

Ponnor shrugged, perhaps indifferently, or perhaps because he understood that there was no other answer possible.

"If I am to remain here, then, I would prefer to work, and not be locked all day in a room."

"We do not lock our boarders in their rooms," protested Friar Julian. "You may walk the halls, or the garden, meditate, read. . ."

"I prefer to work," Ponnor interrupted. "I am accustomed."

Were a boarder to volunteer to work, the agreement between Abbey and police continued, they might do so, without the expectation of compensation.

"If you would like, Friar Tanni will add you to the roster." Friar Julian hesitated, then added, in order that there was no misunderstanding. "Your work would be a gift to this house of the gods."

"I would like," said Ponnor firmly, and, "Yes."

"Then we will see it done," said Friar Julian. A bell sounded, bright and sharp, and he waved Ponnor forward.

"That is the dinner bell. Come along, my child."

* * *

The dining hall was full of people—*gadje*, all. The six friars sat together at one table near the hall door. To these, Niku was made known, and Friar Tanni that moment added him to the lists, and promised to have work for him by meal's end.

He was then released to stand in line, and receive a bowl of broth with some sad vegetables floating in it, a piece of bread the size of his fist, rough, like stone, and as dense, and a cup of strong cold coffee.

This bounty he carried to a long table, and slid onto the end of the crowded bench, next to a yellow-haired *gadje* who looked little more than a boy, and across from a woman who might have been the boy's grandmother.

"You're new," the grandmother said, her eyes bright in their net of wrinkles.

"Today is the first time I eat here," he admitted, breaking the bread and dropping hard pebbles into the soup. "Is the food always so?"

"There's bean rolls, sometimes," the yellow-haired boy said with a sigh. "Bean rolls are good."

"Having food in the belly's good," his grandmother corrected him, forcibly putting him in mind of the *luthia*, the grandmother of all the *kompani*. She looked again to Niku.

"Don't know what we'd do without the friars. They feed who's hungry; patch up who gets sick or broke."

"They do this from their holiness?" Niku asked, spooning up bread-and-broth.

The *gadje* grandmother smiled.

"That's right."

"Some of us," the boy said, "bring finds—from where we're clearing out the buildings don't nobody live in now," he added in response to Niku's raised eyebrows.

"Isn't the same as before, when this was a place for the rich folk," the grandmother said. "When it was over, and those of us who were left—you're too young to remember—" So she dismissed both Niku and her grandson

"Well, I don't mind telling you, I was one thought the friars would leave with the ones who could—and some did. But some stayed, all of them hurting just as much as we, and they opened up the door, and walked down the street, and said they'd be bringing food, soon, and was there anybody hurt, who they could help."

She glanced away, but not before Niku had seen tears in her bright eyes.

"Wasn't anything they could do for my old man, not with half a partment house on top him, but others, who they could."

Niku nodded, and spooned up what was left of his soup. After a moment, he picked up his cup and threw the coffee down his throat like brandy.

The grandmother laughed.

"Not from around here," she said. "Or you'd be going back for more of that." She looked to her grandson.

"You done?"

"Yes, ma'am."

"Then come on."

The boy rose nimbly and went to her side to help her rise. Then the two of them moved off, the boy supporting the grandmother, which was Bedel-like. Niku sat very still, caught with a sudden longing for the sight of his own grandmother.

When it had passed, he rose, and went to find Friar Tanni.

#

His assigned work was to wash the floor in the big room—what the *gadje* called *the nave*. This suited him well, since the door to the street outside stood open during day-hours, and *gadje* of all description were free to come inside, to wander, to sit or lie down for an hour on one of the wide couches, to partake of the offered food.

It was this continual passage of feet that dirtied the nave floor, and Friar Tanni had told him that he might wash it every day, if he wished.

For the moment, he wished, for Fada, when he came, would surely enter by the day-door. It would be best were Niku near at hand to greet him. He had no clear idea what the friars would do, if they found a stranger wandering their halls in search of his brother, but there was, so Niku believed, no reason to discover the truth.

So, he washed the floor, simple work, and soothing, as simple work so often was. When he was done, he took his broom down the long hall to the left of the nave.

This was filled with cabinets, shelves, and tables, and those were filled with this and that and the other thing—an unrelated jumble of objects and intent that vividly brought to mind the work spaces of his brothers and sisters. The "finds" these must be, with which the *gadje* boy and others like him repaid the god-house for its holy care of them.

Dust was thick on surfaces and objects alike, but Niku had the means to deal with that.

He used the broom first, to clean the dusty floor. When that was done, he pulled the duster from the broom's handle, and addressed the collection.

Taking care to keep an eye on the nave, in hope of seeing Fada, Niku set himself to methodically dust the objects.

It was an interesting collection, to put it no higher that its due. One piece he picked up, his fingers curling covetously around it; another he could scarcely bring himself to touch. Valuable, dangerous, fascinating. . .all jumbled together without regard for utility or merit. It was as if the friars did not know what they had, nor how best to make use of it.

Niku had been born after the earthquake and the storm that had destroyed the city, but he had learned from the tales told by his elders. He learned how those who had means had fled, leaving behind those who suffered, and also much of their own property. The Bedel, scavengers and craftsmen, had recovered items similar to those here, in order to repair, destroy, or dream upon them, as each required.

A bell rang, startling Niku, as if from a dream. He walked out of the transept, into the nave, and looked about. There were a number of people about, as there had been, none of them was Fada, which saddened him. If the bell was a call of some kind, it had no power over those in the nave.

Well enough.

Niku returned to the transept.

#

Some time later, and Fada still not with him, he took the broom and duster, which would explain his presence, if he were found where he ought not to be, and explored further.

The South Transept was much like the North, save not yet so full of treasure. He did not pause there, but ascended a flight of stairs, to a loft which was very full of dust, and a standing desk facing a tiered platform. There was a low rail behind the desk and Niku stepped up to look below.

A wondrous sight met his eyes—a device he had only seen in dreams, brass glittering in the muted sunlight admitted by tall soot-stained windows. He stood for a long moment, wonder slowing his heart, then setting it to pounding.

Dazzled, he put one booted foot up on the rail, meaning to make the jump to the floor below.

He stopped himself as he leaned forward to grasp the rail, withdrew his foot, and rushed down the stairs.

A moment later, he crossed the threshold into the sunlit niche—and paused, gazing up at it, its perfect form haloed; light running liquid along the silver pipes.

Softly, Niku mounted the dais.

Gleaming dark wood was like satin beneath his fingers, the bone keys were faintly rough. There was no dust on wood or keys; the brass stops had recently been polished.

Niku sat on the bench and looked over the three tiered keyboards, matching the reality before him with his dreams. Reverently, he extended a hand and touched the brass knobs of the stops, pulling one for each keyboard, those being named the Choir, the Great, and the Swell. He placed his feet on the pedals; leaned in and placed his fingers so upon the Choir keyboard, pressed, and. . .

. . .nothing happened.

Fool, Niku told himself; there will be a switch, to wake the blower.

He found a small brass button set over the Choir, and slightly to the left of center, and pressed it. Then, as memory stirred a little more robustly, he located the *mute* stop, and engaged that, as well.

He pressed his fingers once more against the keys.

Nothing happened.

Frowning, Niku closed his eyes, striving to call up a more detailed recollection of the organ and its workings. It was several long minutes before he opened his eyes again, rose from the bench and descended to the floor.

The trap was behind the organ set flush to the boards.

Niku pulled it up, and sat on his heels, looking down into the dimness. Unlike the instrument, the rungs of the ladder were furry with dust, and likely treacherous footing. He had reached to his pocket before he recalled that the *garda* had taken his light-stick, along with the papers his clever sister Ezell had made for Ponnor Kleug, his *gadje* name.

For another moment he crouched there, debating with himself. Then, with regretful care, he closed the trap, stood—and froze.

He had heard a step, nearby.

Quickly, he ducked out from behind the organ, and went up the dais, pulling the duster from his pocket.

The steps came nearer, and in a moment Friar Julian came into the niche.

He paused for a moment, startled, as Niku read it, to see someone in this place, engaged in admiration of this instrument. Niku smiled.

"It is very beautiful," he said.

The *gadje's* worn face lit with pleasure.

It is," he agreed, coming up the dais to stand at the organ's opposite side, "very beautiful, yes. Sadly, it is not functional."

"Has she ever shared her voice?"

The friar frowned, then smiled, as softly as a young man speaking of his lover.

"Yes. Oh, yes. Years ago now, she. . .shared her voice often. I was, myself, the organist, and—" He shook his head, bereft of words, the soft lips twisted, and the sad eyes wet. "She was damaged in the earthquake. I fear that I will never hear her voice again, on this side of the gods' long river."

"Perhaps," Niku suggested, softly, "a miracle will occur."

Friar Julian's eyes narrowed, and he glared at Niku, who kept his face innocent and his own eyes wide. After a moment, the old *gadje* sighed, and gave a nod, his anger fading.

"Perhaps it will. We must trust the gods. Still, even silent, she—she is a wonder. Would you care to see more?"

"Yes," said Niku.

#

They toured the pipe room, descending the stairs to the blower room, with no need of the trap and ladder. Niku inspected everything; he asked questions of Friar Julian, who was sadly ignorant of much of the organ's inner functions. For the old *gadje*, Niku realized, it was the voice, the opening of self into another self, that mattered. The mechanics, the why, and the what—they did not compel him as they did Niku.

Some while after, they came through the door, back to the organ niche. Niku smiled and bowed his head and thanked the friar for his time.

The sun was low by then, and Niku hurried out to the nave, to see if Fada had come.

#

Fada had *not* come before day had surrendered to night, and the day-door closed and locked. That was. . .worrisome. He depended upon Fada, to bring him, quickly, away.

Niku shared the evening meal of a protein bar and a cup of wine with the friars and the laymen. To take his mind from worry, he listened intently to all they said.

They forgot he was there, tucked into the corner of the table, and they spoke freely. The *garda's* money was to go for medicines. Where they were to find money for food, that was a worry.

A very great worry.

The simple meal done, the *gadje* joined hands, and prayed together, as brothers might do.

After, Friar Julian stood, and the rest, also, and filed off to their rooms. Niku rose, too, and went to the room he had been shown.

There, he showered, his worries filling his belly like so many iron nails. The message that had come to the *kompani* had not been specific as to time, but it was certain that their ship was approaching. What, indeed, if it had already come, and he was left here, along among *gadje*—

He raised his face into the stream of cleansing spray, and with difficulty mastered his panic.

The Bedel did not leave one of their own among *gadje*. Ezell, Fada—the *luthia*—they would not hear of such a thing. They *would not* leave him alone among *gadje*, not while Bedel knives were sharp. He knew that; and it comforted him.

But, still, a man would wish to continue his life, as long as it might joyfully be done.

His best hope yet rested upon Fada. But hope mended no engines.

It is said, among the Bedel, that gods help those who help themselves.

Accordingly, Niku stripped the blanket from the soft, *gadje* bed, wrapped himself in it, and lay down on the floor.

Arms beneath his head, he closed his eyes, and breathed in that certain way that the *luthia* had taught him. And so slid into the place of dreams.

* * *

The accounts page was bathed in red.

Friar Julian sighed, and shook his head, his heart leaden.

A shadow passed over his screen, and Friar Julian looked up, startled.

"Yes, Ponnor?"

The stocky man ducked his unkempt head.

"Friar, I come to offer a bargain, if you will hear it."

Friar Julian frowned.

"A bargain? What sort of a bargain?"

Ponnor stroked the air before him, as if it were a cat—perhaps the motion was meant to soothe him—and said, slowly, "I am an artificer, very fine, and I have studied many devices, including such a device as your lady organ in the niche." He leaned forward, his hands still, black eyes hypnotic.

"I can fix her."

Fix—? Friar Julian's heart leapt painfully in his breast. But surely, he thought, around the pain, surely that was impossible. The earthquake. . .they had done all they knew. . .and yet—

"An artificer?" he said, faintly.

Ponnor nodded. "My brothers—all of us—there is *nothing* that we cannot repair, sir," he said, with a matter-of-factness far more compelling than any more humble declaration.

"And you believe you can repair my—the Abbey's organ."

"Oh, yes, sir," Ponnor assured him. "But there is a price."

Of course there was a price. The gods themselves charged a price, for admission into the Life Everlasting. Friar Julian took a breath, careful of the pain in his breast. The price named by the gods was a soul. Perhaps Ponnor would ask less.

"What is this bargain?" he asked, speaking as calmly as he could.

"I fix your lady organ, and you release me, to return to my grandmother," Ponnor said, and rocked back on his heels, his hands folded before him.

The price was a soul, after all.

Friar Julian swallowed.

He could not, *could not* free Ponnor from his bonds. The chip implanted in his throat would activate and render him unconscious if he moved outside the field of the device locked into the safe in the nave. The police were not idiots, after all; they held the key to the safe; they held the code to the chip.

It was not in Friar Julian's power to release Ponnor to his grandmother, or to anyone else.

But. . .tears rose to his ears. To hear his organ, once more? To play—did he *remember how* to play? Absurd doubt. He played every night, in his dreams.

He could not agree to this. He—

Stay. Ponnor offered his work to the house of the gods and their consorts. That had already been agreed upon. This other thing—what harm, if it gave him some ease while he worked? After all, the police would surely be back soon, to take him before the judge.

Friar Julian took a breath and met Ponnor's black, compelling eyes.

"After you repair the gods' organ, I will release you," he said steadily.

One side of Ponnor's mustache lifted, as if it hid a half-smile, and he continued to hold Friar Julian's gaze for a long, long moment. . .

. . .before he bowed his head, murmured, "I will begin now," and swept from the office.

Friar Julian, abruptly alone, covered his face with his hands.

* * *

Fada arrived as the sun was sinking. Niku had come out of the organ niche to clean the floor in the nave, seeking to ease muscles cramped by long hours of kneeling inside small places, and saw his brother enter, sidestepping those day-folk who were already leaving.

His brother saw him instantly, and raised a hand to adjust his hat, the smallest finger wiggling, which was a request to meet somewhere private.

Niku fussed with the duster, and the broom, in between which his fingers directed his brother to the inner garden, and warned him it would be some time before Niku could join him. He then turned his back and reactivated the broom, in order to clean up a spot of mud that had dried on the floor since his morning pass.

When he looked 'round again, Fada was gone.

\#

Niku had taken a battered lantern from among the clutter in the North Transept to light him on his way. He found Fada lying on a bench under a fragrant tree, hat over his face, snoring.

"Wake, foolish one!" Niku said, slapping his brother's knee. "How if I had been the *garda*?"

"For the *garda*, I am only a man who came to the house for the meal, and fell asleep in the garden," Fada said, swinging his legs around and sitting up.

"I cannot work here," he added, "even with the lantern."

"That is why we are not staying here. Come, Brother; let me show you some things that I found."

\#

"This," Fada said, some minutes later, placing his hand reverently on the organ's polished wood. "*This*, Brother, is something, indeed! Has it a voice?"

"Not presently," said Niku, from his seat on the dais.

"That's too bad." Fada stroked the wood once more, then turned and sat down next to Niku. He reached into his pocket and brought out a flat black rectangle, which he proceeded to unfold until it was a smaller, flatter black rectangle, with various protrusions, like the segmented legs of a river crab.

"First, I take readings," he said, straightening and re-bending the legs. "After I have read, we will know how to proceed, which will we do. You will eat breakfast with your brothers, Niku!"

Hope made him giddy. Fada was the cleverest of his very clever brothers; surely no device of mere *gadje garda* could outwit him. Was it not said of the Bedel—admittedly, by the Bedel—that there was nothing they could not fix, nor any trap that could hold them long?

Fada placed one of the legs against Niku's neck, over the new, pink scar.

"Be still, now—no talking, no moving. Do not *breathe* until I say!"

Niku closed his eyes and held his breath. He heard a high, poignant hum, which might have been the device, or only his ears, ringing from tension.

"*And* breathe," Fada commanded.

This Niku did, reaching up to scratch at the scar.

"Now what do we do?" he asked, when Fada had been silent for what seemed too long.

There was no answer, his brother continuing to stare at the face of his device, his own showing lines of what might be worry.

"Fada?" Niku touched his shoulder.

His brother shook his head, and raised his eyes.

"Niku—Brother, I cannot. . ."

"Cannot?" he repeated. "But—"

"This—thing. It is. . .In a word, Brother, it is beyond me."

"You cannot remove it?"

"That—no. It appears to have established tentacles, and those have intertwined with nerves in your throat. It can never be removed."

Niku felt his stomach churn; the thought of this *gadje* device forever a part of him was enough to make him vomit. He swallowed, hard, and looked back to Fada.

"But you *can* disarm it," he said.

"That—yes. But at risk of your life. I may. . .I will need our brother Boiko for this. . ." His voice faded out, which meant he was thinking.

Niku sat, thinking his own thoughts. Boiko meant frequencies. Frequencies meant there was a way to turn the blessed thing *off.*

"We have heard again," Fada said, interrupting his thoughts, "from the ship. We have a day and a location."

Niku's mouth dried.

"What day?"

Fada looked at him bleakly. "Two days beyond a world-week."

"Surely Boiko can find the frequencies. . ."

"Surely he can, but if we must build a device, in among the packing of all the dreams and findings, for the ship. . ." His face firmed. "We will do it. Brother, you must trust us."

"You are my brothers," Niku said. "But, if Boiko can find the frequencies, we have here a device, Brother." He flung his hand out, showing Fada the organ.

His brother considered the organ over his shoulder, then turned back.

"You said it had no voice."

"And so it does not. But I will fix that."

Fada's face did not lose its expression of worry.

"I don't say that you cannot, Brother, but can it be done in time?"

"It must be done in time," Niku said firmly, "and so it will be."

Fada took a breath. "If you say it, then it is so."

Niku nodded. "And we have another path, Brother. I have a bargain with the *gadje* who loves this organ. When I fix it, he will free me."

"Has he this power?"

"It may be. The *garda* have sealed the control box into a safe. I think that Friar Julian is not a man who allows such things into the gods' house unless he has some measure of control over them."

Niku straightened, and looked at Fada with a surety he did not entirely feel.

"Boiko will find the frequencies. I will repair this organ for the gadje. You will bring the frequencies—in three day's time."

"Three days!"

"Three days," Niku said firmly. "By then, she will have her voice."

"And if it does not?"

"Then there are still seven days left for my brothers to build their device."

A bell rang somewhere in the Abbey, and they fell silent.

Niku then took Fada by the arm and brought him to his feet.

"Come, there is something else you should see."

#

"More treasure, Brother," said Fada, overlooking the tables in the North Transept. Do they know what they hold, these *gadje*?"

"I think not," said Niku. He stepped over to a particular table and held his hand over that object that had so concerned him. "What do you think of this, Brother?"

Fada stepped up beside him and considered the thing with a critical eye.

"I think that it ought to be destroyed. Of course, they don't know how."

"That would be my guess. It ought not to be sitting here where it can work mischief. Will you take it, when you go?"

"It's best, I think," said Fada, and reached into his pocket, producing a muffling cloth, in which he wrapped the thing, before slipping it into a pouch and sealing the top. "That will keep it."

"There is also," Niku said, reaching carefully into a glass cabinet, "this."

Fada pursed his lips in a whistle, and held out his hand.

Niku shook his head.

"You must do another thing for me, Brother. You must sell this at good terms—bargain hard!—and bring me the money, when you return with the frequencies."

Fada frowned.

"Money?" he asked, doubtfully, as who would not? The Bedel did not have much to do with money.

"Money," Niku said firmly.

Fada shrugged and accepted the little figurine, wrapping it also with care and stowing it in an inside, padded, pocket. Then, he looked about.

"Brother, I will stay here until the door opens, and then I will be gone. What will you?"

Doubtless more of the collection would find its way into Fada's pockets, but that hardly gave Niku a qualm. What the Bedel found belonged to the Bedel. It had always been so.

"I will go back to the organ," said Niku.

"Should I come?"

"I think not."

Niku embraced his brother.

"Go safely," he said.

"We will not leave you alone," Fada said, and hugged him hard

* * *

Ponnor was at the organ every waking hour, and Friar Julian suspected, every hour that he ought to be sleeping, too.

The man's diligence shamed Friar Julian—and how much more shame would he feel, he wondered, if Ponnor did restore the organ? When he had first come to Godsmere Abbey, as a boy, he had an elder brother—one Friar Fen. Among the many pieces of wisdom Friar Fen had given his young brother was this—that priests have no honor, for they must always, and first, do everything in their power to serve, without fault, the gods and their consorts. And then they must serve, without fault, those who needed their care the most.

It was not honor, then, that prompted Friar Julian's search of the file cabinets, table drawers, and bookshelves, looking for the key to the constable's safe in the nave.

Surely, he had once had it; therefore, he must have it still. He had given his word, that he would free Ponnor, should he succeed in repairing the organ. Given his word, in this house, where the gods allowed no man to sin.

Late in the night of the second day—or, more accurately, early in the morning of the third—he found it—stuck to the back of the top drawer of his desk. He gripped it in trembling fingers and went out to the nave to test it.

It was only after he stood in front of the safe that he recalled that the police had also applied a sealant, and had taken care to warn Ponnor of its danger.

And for that, he had no answer.

#

"Friar Julian?"

He started from a doze behind his desk and looked up to find Ponnor in the door. His heart took up a hard, sluggish beat that made him feel ill.

"Yes, my son?"

"It is done," Ponnor told him, black eyes fairly sparkling. "She sings again."

The words—it seemed as though he had heard the words, but lost their sense immediately. The organ—what?

"Friar? Will you come?" Ponnor held out his hand.

He sent a prayer to the gods and their consorts, and rose from his chair, willing shaking knees to support him.

"Of course I will come," he said.

#

He sat on the bench, placed his feet on the pedals, and rubbed his cold hands against each other. Ponnor stood next to the organ, at his left, and he was pulling a much folded sheet of paper out of his pocket, which he unfolded onto the wood, and smoothed with his palm.

"Here," he said. "This is a song that I write in celebration of her voice. If you will play this, Friar? I will stand—" He looked over his shoulder and pointed, seemingly at random, "there."

"Even muted, that will be far too close for the safety of your ears, my child."

Ponnor gave him a wide grin, his eyes seeming, in Friar Julian's judgment just a little *too* bright. But, still, the work he had put in to this, the hours of labor and the several nights short of sleep—such things might push a man to frenzy, especially if he labored in a house of gods.

"Please, you will play this?" Ponnor asked again.

Father Julian had long planned what he would play, should the organ ever be repaired, and it grieved him, a little, to cede pride of place to an inept bit of music scribbled onto a grubby sheet by—
By the man he had lied to, and was about to betray.
Friar Julian picked up the paper, running his eye over the notes.
"Of course, I will play this first," he said.

* * *

Niku hurried to the front of the organ, pushing the stops into his ears as he did. When he reached the place Fada and Boiko had determined to be the best, he turned into the sound, and deliberately relaxed.

It was, he thought, a very beautiful thing, this organ. It had been a good thing to do, to repair the blower that had been broken in the quake, and reseat the pipes that had been shaken loose. Very simple repairs. A child could have made them.

Well. Whatever happened in the next few heartbeats—and Boiko himself warned that the outcome might not be happy—he had done well here. This was a deed the memory of which he would wear like a star upon his brow, when he passed to the World Beyond.

Beneath the floor, he heard the blower start.

He heard Friar Julian shift on the bench.

Niku closed his eyes.

The first note sounded, flowed into the second, the third, ascended to the fourth—

Niku felt a jolt of pain, a burning along his throat, he gasped, his hand leaping to the spot. . .

The organ went on. The skin of his throat felt normal, save for the roughness of the scar under his fingers.

Friar Julian played on to the end of the little piece of music Ezell had composed from Boiko's frequencies.

There was a small pause, as perhaps Friar Julian adjusted the stops.

The organ burst into song; a wild, swinging music that had much in common with the music the Bedel made for themselves, when there were no *gadje* to hear.

His feet twitched into a half-step. He laughed at himself, realized that his ears were ringing, despite the stops, and stepped away from the organ.

* * *

Friar Julian frowned at the scrap of music Ponnor had left, his eye moving over the lines. There was something—a progression, a linkage of line and tone. . .

It was, he understood suddenly, a test pattern; a technical exercise, and no music at all.

He smiled, pressed the blower key, and the mute, and placed his fingers on the keys.

The pattern completed, he paused only to set the stops, his hands moving on their own, surely, no shaking now, and he leaned into the keyboards with a will

He had planned. . .For years, he had planned to play the stately and glittering *Hymn of Completion*, which celebrates unions of all kinds, but is most particularly played when one man and another have chosen to pledge themselves to each other for the rest of their mortal lives.

What flowed out of his fingers, however, was not the structured elegance of the *Hymn*, but the provocative and lusty *Dance of the Consorts*.

Friar Julian closed his eyes and allowed his fingers to have their way.

#

He came to an end, and lifted his fingers from the keys, listening to the final reverberations from the pipes. He sighed, his heart full, and his soul healed.

"Friar?" a voice said, very close to his left elbow.

Hearing it, his soul shattered again, and when he turned his head to meet Ponnor's eyes, his own were filled with tears.

The other man smiled.

"I am sorry that I will not be able to stay and hear the rest of the great music," he said. "My grandmother calls me."

Friar Julian shook his head.

"I bargained in bad faith. I cannot release you."

Incredibly, Ponnor's smile grew wider.

"I think you are too hard on yourself," he said, and extended a large, calloused hand. "Come, let us celebrate this lady and her return to song."

Friar Julian hesitated, staring from hand to face.

"Did you understand what I said?" he asked. "It's not in my power to release you."

"That!" Ponnor said gaily. "We will see about that, I think! Come, now, and walk with me. We will test this thing. Let us go together down the street to the tavern. We will drink, and bid each other farewell."

"I tell you, it is impossible!" cried Friar Julian.

His wrist was caught in one large hand, and he came to his feet, reluctantly, and Ponnor's hand still holding him, went out of the niche and into the nave, where the day visitors and the laymen, and all of the friars, stood, their faces bathed in wonder.

"Was that," asked a woman wearing a flowered apron, "the organ?"

"Julian?" said Friar Anton. "Is it—I thought I heard. . ."

"You did hear!" Ponnor answered, loudly. "Your organ sings again! Soon, Friar Julian will come back and play for you all, but first, he and me—we have business to conduct."

No one questioned him, least of all Friar Julian, the music still ringing in his head. The crowd parted before them, all the way down to the day-door.

Friar Julian came to his wits as the sun struck his face, and he pulled back.

"You will be struck!" he cried.

"Not I!" Ponnor declared. "What a beautiful day it is!"

That was so, Friar Julian saw, the sun smiling cheerfully upon the broken street, and the children playing Find Me! among the piles of salvage.

Halfway down the street, the bright red sign of the saloon mere steps ahead, Friar Julian exclaimed, "But you're out of range! The chip should have activated!"

"You see?" Ponnor grinned. "You have kept your word! The gods of the house would not let you sin."

A miracle, thought Friar Julian. I am witness to the movements of the gods.

Dazed, he followed Ponnor into the room, and allowed him to choose a table near the door.

"Sit, sit! I will fetch us each a glass of blusherrie! A special day begs for a special drink!"

The friar sat, and glanced about him. The hour was early and custom was light. Across from him a dark haired man wearing a hat sat alone at a table, nursing a beer. On the other side of the door, near to the bar, a young woman with red ribbons plaited into her black hair, black eyes sultry, sat by herself, an empty glass on the table beside her.

"Here we are!" Ponnor returned noisily, placing two tall glasses of blue liquid in the table's center, as he sat down in the chair opposite.

"We will drink to the lady's restored health!" Ponnor declared, and they did, Friar Julian choking a little as the liquid burned down his throat. It had been a long time since he had drunk such wine.

"We will drink to the wisdom and the mercy of the gods and their consorts!" he cried then, entering into the spirit of the moment.

They drank.

"We will drink to fond partings," Ponnor said, and they did that, too.

Father Julian sighed, surprised to see that his glass was nearly empty. He felt at peace, and more than a little drowsy.

Across the table, Ponnor set aside his glass and rose.

"I leave you now," he said. Father Julian felt his hand lifted, and blinked when Ponnor placed a reverent kiss upon his knuckles.

"Enjoy your sweet lady, sir," Ponnor said, and was gone, walking briskly out the door.

At once, the man and the woman at the single tables rose and followed him out.

That was odd, thought Friar Julian, and sleepily raised his glass for another sip of blusherrie.

"Hey," said a rough voice at his side. Friar Julian blinked awake and smiled sleepily up at a man wearing an apron. The barkeeper, perhaps.

"Yes?" he said.

"What I wanna know," the man said, looking down at him with a thunderous frown, "is who's gonna pay for them drinks."

Friar Julian sat up straight, suddenly and vividly awake.

Money! He had no money! Ponnor—

"The guy with the mustache said you'd pay for them, too," the barkeep said, using a blunt thumb to indicate the two single tables, now empty. "We ain't the church, here, see? You drink, you pay."

"Yes, I understand," said Friar Julian, his heart sinking, thinking of the few coins left in the cash box, after the medical supplies had been purchased.

Futilely, knowing they were empty, he patted the pockets of his robe. The right one was as flat as he expected, but the left one. . .

Crinkled.

Wondering, Friar Julian pulled out a bright blue envelope. He ran his finger under the flap, and drew out a sheaf of notes. Notes! Not coins.

He offered the topmost to the bartender, who eyed it consideringly.

"Hafta go in back to change that," he said.

Friar Julian nodded.

Alone, he fanned the money, seeing food, medicines, seeds for their kitchen garden. . .

Something fluttered out of the envelope. Friar Julian bent and picked it up off the floor.

It was a business card for one Amu Song, dealer in oddities, with an address at the spaceport. Father Julian flipped it over, frowning at the cramped writing there.

The gods help those who help themselves.

He stared at it, flipped the card again, and there was the word, *oddities*. He thought of the North Transept, the cluttered tables of worthless offerings there.

...and he began, very softly, to laugh.

About the Authors

Maine-based writers Sharon Lee and Steve Miller teamed up in the late 80s to bring the world the story of Kinzel, a inept wizard with a love of cats, a thirst for justice, and a staff of true power. Since then, the husband-and-wife team have written dozens of short stories, and twenty-one novels, most set in their star-spanning Liaden Universe®. Before settling down to the serene and stable life of a science fiction and fantasy writer, Steve was a traveling poet, a rock-band reviewer, reporter, and editor of a string of community newspapers. Sharon, less adventurous, has been an advertising copywriter, copy editor on night-side news at a small city newspaper, reporter, photographer, and book reviewer. Both credit their newspaper experiences with teaching them the finer points of collaboration. Sharon and Steve passionately believe that reading fiction ought to be fun, and that stories are entertainment. Steve and Sharon maintain a web presence at www.korval.com

For a complete list of Lee and Miller eChapbooks, please visit Pinbeam Books (www.pinbeambooks.com)

Thank you

for your interest in
and support of
our work
Sharon Lee and Steve Miller

Made in the USA
San Bernardino, CA
12 September 2017